Contents

The Wraith

A fountain of cold brick
Surrounded by solemn sticks separated
From their parent tree
That is what I see
Hear before me
And I feel so wonderfully
A sense of secluded solidarity

Ah, but 'tis not observed so simply
For around this fountain rest quietly
With no question or quandary
These quaint shops which are so sexy
They blur together so perfectly
Undoubtedly
Not accidentally
And the sun sets distantly
Dipping oh so very carefully
Into the milky lavender sea
Ah yes, that is what I see
Hear before me
And I feel so terribly
A sense of second finality

I crane my neck continually
Gazing and scoping hurriedly
The sights surrounding me
Searching for that which I knew would be
Waiting here eternally
For me, and only me

Then as I see
I begin here to hear loudly
The sordid sobbing of eternity
The black tentacles coil menacingly
Yet coincidentally and simultaneously
Also beg innocently
For forgiveness is not given or received easily

The wraith sits upon the edge of this fountain silently
Writhing with fear wrought upon it repeatedly
Although quite undoubtedly and ironically
It is the cause of the same fear that cripplingly
Petrifies all those who dare to see
This black pulsing creature crawling through eternity
Write here in front of me

That is what I see
Hear before me
And I feel so painfully
A sense of loss so deeply

So as my trepidations subside and slip slowly
And no longer insist on subsisting incessantly
Like busy buzzing bees
Around the hive protecting the queen
I begin to approach the wraith reluctantly

If you will allow me
To tangent momentarily
And use nouns as verbs incorrectly
Then you may see
How standing here I came to be

It is a tale best told over tea
But the time to make some is not ready
So let us settle for a potion from the apothecary
Ah yes, that very same apothecary
That cunningly convinced me
That this wraith would be waiting for me
Wanting to reveal to me
A secret about me

Do not fear and want greedily
As you now read confusedly
For I am returning fearlessly
To my encounter with this wraith waiting for me
As the sun is setting silently
Into the shimmering sea
And yet casts no shadows I can see

My advance toward it is halted immediately
I am trapped in an invisible grip so steely
That I feel icy knives gripping me
Snakes coiling around me
Ants scurrying purposefully
Up my legs in a hurry

The fountain begins flooding freely
Spilling the water wickedly
Splashing a mist upon me
Quite comfortingly
That is what I see

Hear before me
And I feel so overwhelmingly
Deadly

Now I see a link of causality
Between the presence of this thing before me
And the pain that is caused to me
For you see
Before I noticed eternity
Or even let myself believe
That such future could be
I did not exist painfully
But rather peacefully

So I strive to find the identity
Of this wraith that curses me
So very cruelly
And quite intelligently
Although very regrettably
I look down at the water that is now to my knees
And hope to discern in reflexivity
The face of eternity

Rewarded is my futility
For shockingly though not surprisingly
The reflection of the wraith is me

That is what I see
Hear beneath me
And as the tears begin to flow and add to the pool below me
I feel quite simply
The pull of gravity

The Mirror

I sat frantic
Upon the wooden floor of my attic
Though I should say
However important this fact may
Appear to be
It was indeed a cold day in May
And supposedly
As you may

Have already deduced
Or perhaps not maybe
As you may not be the sleuth
That I suspect you to be

In this attic in which with every breath I made dust scatter
The month, week, day, hour, minute, second
Did not truly, or even slightly, matter
Everything slurred together so elegantly
That it could make even the most obsessive compulsive person cringe
Although not quite racially
The slurring still softly said some biting things

But it is not about this attic that I write
Though it is always appropriate in my mind
To set the scene for such a plight
It is about this glass door
That I sat staring into for hours
A door that can only best be described as a whore
Sucking the innocence from weak cowards
That I sit down with pen and paper today
To attempt to explain away

I think here to myself at this juncture
Not staring at, but in, reflection
Where does a door's power come from?
And my wandering mind answers in perfection
Well, the power comes from people entering and exiting
To and from
The swing of the pendulum

Consider then this thing
I say to my mind as it returns
From its journey, or maybe more of a fling
Why then does my soul so violently churn?
Why does the grip of this glass door burn?

If the handle I haven't so much as turned?

My mind is silent
It's about time
That damned thing should repent
For all of its crimes

Now I return reluctantly
To my previous inquiry
Of the nature and source of power
Of this whore of a door that prays upon cowards
Ah, there is indeed an answer
A door's power, you must see
Does not come from exit and entry
No, it comes from the opportunity
For you must agree
That while entering Hell is terrible
Having to do it after being promised Heaven
Must be far more unbearable
And continually
A broken heart definitely hurts
But if it breaks from betrayal
The pain is probably far worse
Yet even more so
The death of a child is no easy thing
But if it is unexpected in infancy
There may indeed be a sharper sting

So you must realize
The evidence is ample
That when into the water you dive
The fall isn't quite so simple

So then allow me to continue my address
For alas, I feel I may have digressed
Let us now return
To that door with the grip that burns

It is quite clear, at least to me
That the power of a door
Comes from its entrancing ability
To make people believe
That there is something else in store
I suppose that it is this grip
That is what really
In the end, managed to get me

For in that night in May
As I sat staring at the fray
That the glass did spray
I could not help but appreciate
What can I say?
The self is a commodity that doesn't depreciate

For by now you must have guessed
Unless you are an idiot
Which I did not suspect
That this door is actually not
It is a far greater horror
This door is an old mirror
You may even be slightly
Sitting silently in anger at me
That I spent such time on this analogy
I assure you though it was not a waste
For it gives you a taste
Of the simple truth that even reflection
Has the same power of seduction
That same uncanny ability
To make a person believe
In what could maybe possibly be
Some different enticing reality
So much like a door
This mirror too is quite the whore
And maybe you will not in anger curse
When you realize this verse
Does in fact have some sort of purpose

But now I grow weary
My eyes begin to grow teary
So then please respectfully
Allow me
To reach quickly
The end of my time
In front of this mirror

I allowed myself for a second to think
That perhaps there was indeed something
In what I saw looking back at me
But it was a foolish belief
For I know now that what stared back at me
Was very simply
Empty

Caught up in possibility
Thinking that maybe that person may matter
I reached toward the reflection reluctantly
Only to witness the mirror shatter

To this day I still sit
Trying vainly to rebuild
That destroyed person
That helped me cope
That gave me some little hope
Though I conduct my efforts vainly
And I am so incredibly lonely
And I am hoping
That someone comes visiting after reading
This message I am sending
But to those wandering
I issue this single warning

That upon arriving
In this place of mourning
There is no escaping

Hanging

Drowning
Breathing
The former involves the cessation of the latter
It is quite a simple matter

Blinding
Seeing
The former involves the cessation of the latter
It is quite a simple matter

I often sit thinking, wondering, pondering
Over many uncertain things
Though there is one particular musing
Upon which I am now sitting

The bubbles around me rising
Their wobbling shells popping
The green swell swirling
The emeralds sparkling

Before I continue alarming
You as you are reading
This tale and contemplating
Precisely where I am going

Just sit quietly and continue listening
As I begin explaining
How I came to be drowning
Underneath the shattered sunlight so blinding

It is really a simple thing
As I explained when introducing
My state at the beginning
Of this meeting

Though there must be some not so uncertain something
Which catalyzes the stopping
Of this very breathing
And continues initiating
The ending of this very seeing

I found myself running
Through a corridor my vision tunneling
As I increased the speed of my sprinting
I felt the metronome of my heart ticking

Ticking
Ticking
Ticking

Shortness of breath began gripping
My chest as it continued heaving
Every fiber of muscle burning
Under my skin as it continued writhing

Upon my target I was closing
I could feel my torment coming
To a swift ending
As the end of this corridor I was reaching

I saw in the floor a gap gaping
Just waiting
For the next life to come wanting
More and more and never satisfying
Continually desiring

I found myself vaulting
Over this gap that continued extending
Beyond the reach of my most energetic leaping
And as I was sailing
Above this gap that was expanding
I looked below and saw standing
Myself, just standing

That standing self I saw began reaching
His hand up to me as if begging
As I flew over that gap my mind marked one remarkable thing
Upon that reaching hand was dripping
Blood and cooling
The flesh upon which it was gliding

At this sight my fears began rearing
Their fangs began seizing
My consciousness in their seething
Venomous bite and began ripping
My courage and shredding
My resolve until my vigor started fleeting

The door at the end now also began running
With every step I took after the gap it was receding
Farther from me as my breathing

Began ceasing

As I gradually began slowing
My stride and fainting
Onto the ground which began fading
Into nothingness and disappearing
Beneath me it began falling

I grew dim and began collapsing

This is how I came to be floating
And looking up at the light that is blinding
As it is fractured by the waving
Of the pool in which I am drowning

As I am slipping
Deeper and deeper I notice something red swirling
Into the pool mixing
The scarlet so mesmerizing

My gaze awakens and begins frantically searching
For the origin of this red fluid dripping
Into the pool in which I am drowning
Then my gaze finds itself settling

Upon an icy cool hand reaching
Into this abyss and beckoning
For my grip reckoning
That I will not succumb to this drowning

I am tearing
At my will to begin reaching
And grasp the saving
Blood cooled hand that is reaching

It is this dying will
I am now reviving
This blinding drowning
I am now battling

This trial

Is where I am now hanging

The Secret of El Dorado

I was walking once
Along a path
By my goal I had become incensed
And drunk

Intoxicated I stumbled
Beneath my breath I grumbled
My feet bleeding and sore
From carrying this incredible wait that I bore
Certain knowledge, though, of what was in store
Allowed me to continue forever more

Small clouds of dust
Puffed around my aching soles
Each step I took and thought I must
Reach the end to save my soul

The Spaniard, The Ambitious
The Alcoholic Gallant Knight
All had failed in their own renditions
Of this very same fight

Along this dusty path
A traveler I met
As the hot sky
Hammered nails into my bare head

He questioned in deep and sordid tone
My son, where in such haste do you go
To which I replied
Father, it is in search that I go
It is at the end of this path I have come to know
That fabled city of El Dorado

And beneath his black brimmed cap
His eyes began to dance
Grin and enchant
I met his mesmerizing gaze
And began to slip into a sleepy haze

My son, he said carefully to me
Be warned, take care, take heed
For gold, to the ancient ones, did not mean
The same as it does to you and me
Treasure

Was something to them quite different entirely
They knew what it meant to be
A member of the race of humanity
And live truly freely
So treasure, you see
Was therefore something quite different to them
Entirely

To El Dorado I have journeyed
And the secret it holds so dear
I have already seen
It is an evil thing
This greed so consuming
That keeps you going
From yesterday until tomorrow
In search of that fabled El Dorado

I am almost certain that when you find it
You will be quite disappointed
Tell me something child
Why do you go
So brave and so bold
In search of El Dorado?

Growing greater in anger
At having my purposes challenged
I replied so harsh and cold
Foolish old man
Is it not clear why I go
So brave and so bold
In search of El Dorado?
Who would not want to find a city of gold?

At this he began to cackle
And so my heart became shackled
By that thundering cackle

Listen boy!
I have witnessed death and resurrection
And traveled in that very direction
And let me just tell
I have fallen victim to that same vaulting ambition which
O'erleaps itself

I gave no credence to this old wanderer
Clearly the sun had baked him insane

His sensibility no longer remained
So I ceased our palaver

But immediately I became arrested
By a thought
Maybe I should ask just one question
Tell me old man
If you have truly seen the city
El Dorado is down this path, is it not?

He nodded thrice
Then once more gave me the same advice
Indeed boy, the city lies before you
But I must remind you
It is not the same city
That you have imagined it to be
You needn't make the remainder of this journey
Because the secret of the city
Is right in front of you for you to see

Of his blathering I grew weary
As I departed I heard what seemed nearly
To be, at least to me
The old man's last breath

As I drew upon the horizon
His words began to echo
My son, my son, my son
As I continued to go
Toward that fabled city
Of El Dorado

I approached with great anxiety
And excitement all the same
As I came close
I saw broken iron gates
Crippled and lame

I looked to my left
Saw a wall of crumbling brick
Glanced to my right
Saw a wall of crumbling brick

Surely, undoubtedly, this cannot be
The fabled city
Of El Dorado

I stepped in through those gates
And heard the silent metronome
Of aging slate and stone
Around me
Moss covered crumbled columns lay in pieces
Around me
I saw not gold, nor jewels, nor sunshine
Around me
So gloomily and predictably
Echoed the words of that old man
Around me

My mind sought an answer
The world had to answer
For my deeds I had to answer
My questioning journey needed and answer
For it could not just be
That this heap of rubble before me
Was that fabled city
That I had sought so vehemently

The weeping cry of a crow broke the silence
The air grew thick and dense
With the heavy stench
Of disappointment
Suddenly a block fell from the ceiling
Crashing on the floor
The sun shot through beaming
And sought to show me there may be something more

The light situated itself upon something
I came close toward that something
And found some sort of coffin
A large granite circle lid contained the something
My mind began fantasizing about what something
Could lay therein

Larger across than the span of a vulture's wings
Waist high on my body
Was this container that housed
That something

It must be
I thought to myself with glee
It must be

The secret treasure of this city

With all my mustered might
I began the final fight
To unearth this secret
Which had been revealed to me by the light

I struggled and pushed
Turned that lid away
I struggled and pushed
The stone circle tipped over
Fell
And became shattered clay
Overcome by anxiousness
I turned my gaze toward
That something
I had begun this journey in search of

Tears fell so suddenly from my cheeks
Dropped into my eyes there before me
Ripples distorted the reflection
That I saw in the water I had unearthed
Beneath me

The secret the city
Had kept with such veracity
Had kept by consuming the lives of so many
Who had come before me
Was simply
A reflection
In life
That is all it had to show me

I turned and began walking
To finally awaken from this dream
And thankful is all I could be
That I had come to know
Before
I grew in age as old
As that man with the black brimmed cap
Who had warned me

Thankful I was ever so
That I had so early in my life
Come to know
The secret of that fabled city

Of El Dorado

Whispers

If ever you feel that there is nothing more
There is nothing after here and now forever more
Believe in something more
For I have heard secrets from whispers that speak no more

They stood in the corners of my eyes
Swirling and writhing
Waiting in darkness they would lie
Twisting and turning
Into gruesome shapes and forms
Only to torment me
Bringing upon my sanity a storm

They would tell me of suffering that has and will come to pass
Tragedies that would forever last
Terrible things in this life and the life after it
The flaming world, they told me, I would soon inhabit it

I begged and pleaded for them to cease
Their incessant whispering
At every moment of day and night
Their words like daggers

I scraped and clawed

Cried and bawled

To no avail
I took a blade
To my own eyes
In hopes to quiet them

Blindness now takes me
But so does the most beautiful silence

A Letter to My Future Self

I work tirelessly
That you may not have to
I improve relentlessly
In the vain hopes that you will be
Perfect

I drive endlessly
Toward you

I continue to draw breath
To keep the candle of your life burning
I try my best

To construct a world
That you will inherit
And an existence
That you will love

Do not lose sight
Of what led to you
Of who gave to you
Of who braved shattered friendships
Broken hearts

Crippling secrets
The steely grip of the grave
The dark ice of unending winters

All that you may live
Without regrets

Never forget to love yourself
Because sometimes
Even I wonder if I do

Breathe

Doesn't it trouble you?
I know it troubles me
That everything I see
Here, there, and around me
May not even really be
There

Light is fast
Incredibly fast
But fast doesn't mean instant
Even if it did
The now would still be very distant

So I don't know
The days come and go
Yet my flitting sorrow
Never quite sets with the sun
Because as the ebb and flow
Of time trickles below
As I said, I don't know
Exactly where I am
Or where I'm going to go
Or even if I will

They'll tell you to live in the present
You know, those people
Who think they've got it
All figured out
Completely
Entirely
Figured
Out

Strange thing about the here
And Now
You can't actually hear
What's making sound now
Because by the time it gets here
It's already gone....now

They tell you live
In a place and time
Impossibly unreachable
So sit listen, listen
To the chimes

Echo from the steeple
Of time

Let the whispered clouds speak to you
The winding winds gently kiss you
The calming silence grip you
The soft embrace of sleep take you
As you just

Breathe

Warning Unheeded

Into my books my soul pouring
I sat with my caged heart scouring
For some wide open door

Into which I could hope to enter
As this world's sole cold dissenter
And want or desire no more

That is when I began the tumbling fall
My infected mind unable to deny the call
In my chest chains with a lock being tied

So it continued for some several days
As upon me there set a dark and hazy daze
To blind myself from all inquiring eyes

How I can now recall that night so vividly
When the blacksmith ceased his work silently
His hand by something abruptly arrested

The wind had been whipping particularly violent
Over and over, bang bang, the shutters went
Of peace the spirits had been divested

Questioningly quiet I sat, my head in my hands
The stars shining, the constellations cruelly disguised brigands
Trying desperately my focus to steal

The shadows whispered, chattered, and danced
And quickly at the lighted timekeeper I glanced
One, Two, Zero, Zero, all too real

I cannot help but remember every detail
I can only imagine my countenance, how frail
My mind at that point in complete control

She flew in, glided, stumbled, and shined at once
Her eyes, meeting mine, in desperate hunt
I heard it then, the celestial drum roll

No more chains then, as I felt her turn the key
I glanced at her periodically, seeing her glancing back at me
Knowing then that our future something would hold

Then the smith screamed as loud as he could

A warning, to which listening, yet not heeding, I confusedly stood
Her blue darkness, stunningly warm, glaringly cold

She was a hummingbird, little did I know
A frantically fluttering angel, white as newly fallen snow
The padlock tumbled through my ribs with dusty knocks

That moment, the first that I heard from her
So violently my dormant heart then stirred
I hardly had time of myself to take stock

I had long before this meeting been abandoned
By the cold fingers of the heavens, shunned
She gave me back those wings I had lost

I once again ascended to where I had been
Among the galaxies, unscathed, pristine
My sanity, the only cost

So the pendulum then swings
Bringing with it more I cannot understand
Helpless now, the blacksmith's work gone, I stand
And the hushed indefinite whispers continue to sting

Uncertain, unknowing, afraid, I continually fret
As sickeningly, frighteningly, crawls into my heart
A child crippled by defect
I now turn toward this toddler in a start

I see on her chest chained a device
Striking in its similarity to that steel snake that had so soon ago snaked its screaming grasp around mine
Succumbing then to my greatest vice
I kindly asked the nurse to reach around me and hand me my micro-tome

I hardly knew then when I looked at the clock
That when the minute hand struck Eternity
I would still be working to free that child from her chains and lock
I suppose that is the mercifully deadly venom of Destiny

Echoes

Have you heard
The screeching echoes
Their call is like a heard
Of weeping willows

Their cries ring
Through empty hallways
Their whispered ding
Screams always

I sit in the twilight
Wind pressing against my cheek
As I begin to feel the cold embrace of night
I lose my strength and become weak

Then they begin
Singing, ringing, screaming
Taunting, haunting, calling
Peace becomes a flitting feeling

I grasp and claw
Desperately reaching
For my own sanity
That is rapidly fleeting

There is no rest
Or repentance to be had
The echoes shall soon take me
But for that I am glad

It is the power of loneliness that grips me
The isolation of my victories that pushes me
The infinite desire to be seen for what I am
The infinite wisdom to know that I never can

I am reminded by the echoes
And their incessant crying
That I am hidden deep inside myself
And my soul is just silently sighing

They repeat over and over
Their song of solitude
And I cannot shed
But one tear of gratitude

I hold on only to that glimmer
Of small vibrant hope
That soon I will succumb
To their unending grope

In these final moments in which I can see
The sea of the beauty of the world around me
I take my last opportunity
To pray for you that you may live peacefully
And as your life continues to go
You never have to fade
The infinite call
Of the echoes

Drums

The rhythm hums
He hears the constantly beating drums
The angels' chorus has begun
But the light will not overcome

He envies those who can forget
What they have done
Those who live without regret
For all they have done

He cannot
All his effort is for not
In his heart is tied a knot
And he knows not
Whether he shall find salvation from his thoughts

The rhythm of the drums
Burns in his head
And his thoughts turn
Over and over upon what
He has begun

The fault was not his
The angels sing to him
The commands ring to him
Unable to silence the constant din
He reluctantly begins

And on this night the darkness is
Particularly heavy and moonlight
Is darker than it is usually
As he digs, digs so feverishly
To wipe from his memory
What he has done, eternally

As the colors of twilight had sat
Calmly upon the horizon
The angels' chorus had come back
To sing for him a new direction

He was told of the terrible things
She had done
Accusations of crimes
Against him and everyone

As he stared at the last light
Of the setting sun
The gentle violets of the sky
Blended into a fiery red
And his task begun

He rose from his perch
And sought to silence the singing
That commanded him forth
On his errant errand
The command kept ringing

He was there now
And could smell her now
The trail of her scent floated around
He knew that he would do it now

The wolf echoed a morose call
Echoing through the night
Vibrating through the quiet world
Under the watchful moon's light

To the sound of that call
He carried out his task
And that piercing chorus
Was silent at last

But only a moment's respite
Was he reward
The trumpet's call blared
And so did the drums of war

As he digs here
Trying to bury
That which he has wrought
The drums roar
A thunderous and continuous
Rhythm in his chest
Taking over the beating of his heart
And his conscious

As the digging is done
He lifts that tattered memory of his
Devilish deed
And tosses it into the earth
As it tumbles into the dirt

He prays that soon he will have peace
From the rhythm of the drums

But his wishing is in vain
The drums will never cease
Until the trumpet's call sounds
And gives way
For his soul to sail
To the kingdom
From whence the angels came

Home

Howls, screeches, and screams
Slamming doors and crashing glass
Haunt his dreams

Hazily he wanders
Among the muffled shadows
And the reverberating echoes

There is no rest
No sweet balm
To sooth the tugging in his chest

Flashes of memories
Of fists and insults
Thrown back and forth among stories
Of histories that have been forgotten

Tears and tortured turning
Take hold of sleepless nights

Cursing and shouting
Is all he can hear
And all that is in sight

The hallways are damp
Heavy with a want of love
Forever hoping it will come
He looks up in search of the dove

It is a cage
Only few understand
It is a prison
Only the prisoners understand

He closes his eyes as the burn of sadness begins
Tries to escape into his memories and find some resolution
There is only more
His head is a store
Of this, everything he sees before
Him, everyday
Every waking moment he stays
He hopes quietly in solitude
Plans his escape
His flight of final freedom

He pictures that bright morning
As the sun's rays illuminate his body, hanging
His feet turn the clock
From nine to three
Then back again
He'll finally be
Home

My Fault

It must be my fault
It is my birth that wrought
This tortured existence upon them
It is my life that continues
To torture and taunt them

It must be my fault
Every disagreement
Every shout
Every cursing biting word

In that fault I live
That fault is where I exist
The space I occupy in this time
And every time to come to be

I cower in the corner
Of the recesses of my own mind
I shiver and shudder
Caught among these doubts of mine

It must be my fault
So why not remove the fatal flaw
Erase the black mark
Forget that first mistake
Remove it and pretend it never happened

It's a brilliant idea
A plan formed among monsters
And angels alike
A desire destined
To bring me to the devil's side

It's mercy
In its most beautiful form
A message sent
Through the booms of thunderstorms

It's my fault
So I suppose it's my responsibility too
To fix everything that's wrong
To remove that fault
It's what I have to do

With a swift flick

The sunshine's brief glint
The crimson tide swells
Clarity begins to drift

Forgiveness creeps its cold grip around me
As I say goodbye I think finally my last thought
It was my fault

Sleep

Dangerous territory
The fields of her mind
Devoid of serenity
Immune from the passage of time

She shivers and quivers
The heat grips her
Mumbles haunted whispers
As her soul cracks like dry timber

She runs
And runs
Going nowhere
The safety of a comforting hand eluding her
Forever

Memory stitches itself
To terrible memory
Joins itself cleverly
To ghosts of the not so distant past

She is strength
But her strength makes her lonely
In the darkness of the oppressive night
She is the one and only
Passenger of her nightmares

They are a different reality
That she had once lived
Though she found freedom
She still struggles to free herself from that reality's grip

It comes for her every night
Hungry with fangs bare
Galloping after her
It can smell her unending fear

But she is strong
So she perseveres
The daylight peeks through
Her curtains
Illuminates the cool morning air

Her eyes flutter
Her heart shudders

She tumbles
Out of the past
Into the present

The day begins
The waiting game
She goes through the motions
In anxious anticipation
For sleep to take her again

Memory

I'm doomed to repeat it
Whether I'm ignorant
Or aware of it

I'm destined to relive it
Whether I ignore it
Or recognize it

There is no merciful release
From the infinite pull
There is no gracious respite
From the unending grip

Of my memory

The sins I've committed
Those committed against me
Those committed with me
Those committed without me
The sins of others
For which the blame falls on me

The reel plays over and over
Torn celluloid frames of horror
Tear at the backs of my eyes
My sanity is trapped in a corner

The landscape of what I remember
Smokes with the heat
Of wars fought without laws
Or limits
Or care

It's scarred by a the charred remains
Of unforgotten souls
That drift and haunt
Circle my thought and taunt
Me forever with the cries
Of their pain
Of their desire for vengeance
Of their forgiveness

The skies above rain down ash
Grey snowflakes of death and darkness
Staining me as I stand

In the middle of the remnants
Of my life

The air is heavy
Damp and dingy
It warmly stings my sanity
Crushing me

I walk forward but
With every step I take
I only extend my horizon farther
See more of what I have wrought
See more of the pain I have brought
See more of those I have forgotten
Or at least
Tried to forget

So I walk
This never ending land
Of ashes and corpses
Or smoke and deceit
Of hopelessness and carnivorous secrets
On shattered glass
I walk the landscape

Of my memory

Clocks

Tick tock tick tock
The pantomime starts
Tick tock tick tock
The time cannot be forgot

Tick tock tick tock
I dig deeper
Tick tock tick tock
I will be his keeper

They are reminders
Their hands constantly turning
They are rejoinders
To reason's efforts of returning

Tick tock tick tock
My fingers ache
Tick tock tick tock
Salvation is at stake

Tick tock tick tock
Life is running out
Tick tock tick tock
The candle is burning out

The whisper of the song of urgency
The ringing strikes in the air
Speaking a sense of brevity
As I continue to tear

Tick tock tick tock
The darkness is biting at my heels
Tick tock tick tock
The heavy air is becoming real

Tick tock tick tock
They scream now
Tick tock tick tock
I start waking from this dream now

She is teetering on the brink
Suspended in her most perfect moment
I am awakened to every sense
I offer them a small token

Tick tock tick tock
The passage of time slows
Tick tock tick tock
The river no longer flows

Tick tock tick

Of Fire

Some are born and destined
To be only glimmers in the galaxy
They shine briefly and fade
Forgotten for eternity

Some are born and destined
To be nothing more than periods
At the end of a sentence
They make their statements
And are never remembered

Some are never born
They are only wishes
In the whispered prayers
Of a weeping mother
Staring at an empty cradle

But some
Yes, some
Are born to be burned
Into the hearts of the masses
Never to be locked away
In the pages of history
But to burn their souls
Into those very books
That speaks of lands and times long lost
To the ever shifting sands
Of this life we live

They are born enigmas
It is in their eyes
The offspring of gods and demons
Conceived on the brightest of nights

They hunt for power
They thirst for control
They hunger for the fear of cowards
They feed on the weakness of others' souls

Their flesh sears the air around them
Their gaze pierces even the most well-guarded hearts
Their pride is never shallow
Their resilience is unparalleled

Angels bow to them

And devils cower before them
They rule the heavens and the earth
Even after they return
To the fire
From whence they came

A Child's Confession

One cool and calm night
The brightness of the moon howled outside
A weighty calm settled over me

Into a deep sleep I began to slip
As suddenly the wind at my window gave a kick
From my rest the noise tore me

Abruptly a steely fear struck me
I sat straight up and looked about me
There was nothing to be seen

A faint laughter gently kissed me
The origin of which escaped me
And still, there was nothing to be seen

The room was stunningly empty
The last dying embers of the fire crackled quietly
And I sat there, staring stupidly into the emptiness

The patter of footsteps whispered
Sending me into a brief shudder
I saw her standing in front of me

Surely, I said to myself, it cannot be
But surely she stood in front of me
Her beauty completely unchanged

Darling, the word barely escaped my lips
I stuttered, still unable to believe it
I thought she was lost to the angels

She continued to stand in silence
Shimmering and putting me into a trance
I thought it time to ask just what had happened

That night that had thrown my life asunder
That night under lightning and thunder
As I had buried my only daughter

Who was it, I asked hopefully
Tell me please, I begged sorrowfully
Who took you from me?

She continued to stand in silence

My heart sank deeper into my chest
Shivering in my own skin

Sweetheart please, as the tears came
Their heat searing trails into my face
Tell me, you must know!

She rose an arm slowly
Outstretched finger pointed at me
And then my heart truly dropped

No, I moaned at her, it wasn't me
I watered your grave with my tears
Every year since that night

I buried you with grace
A testament to the joy of your life
No, not me, I screamed in silence

Arm still outstretched, she began to turn
Her back to me now, the tears still burned
She pointed at the door to the room

The knob turned slowly, and the door began to open
My daughter disappeared in a wisp of smoke
As my wife walked in

Longing for Daylight

Peace
That is all I want
The sweet release
From everything that haunts
My nightmares
And my dreams
Respite
From everything that hides
In the shadows of my mind

I want to be free
From those twisting corners of darkness
Those jagged screams
Reverberating off broken glass
I want to be blind
From the reflections that surround me
As I walk through the mirrored corridors
Of my thoughts

I step to my window
The curtains flutter
A chill snakes down my back
I shudder

The moon pulses above
Floating just beyond the bony grasp
Of the witch's frail fingers

The breeze gives me a shove
Backwards into the room I stumble
The night has had enough
The wraiths hiss outside
Refusing to let me abide
Refusing to let my shivers subside

I collapse
Sink into the floor
Eyes wide open
I shake and twist
Wondering if I can take anymore

Moon beams sing through the curtains
Peeking through at my writhing form

The pain sharpens

The creatures of the night are strengthened

Their hungry growls thunder through the steely air
I struggle with all my might

To regain control

But I no longer have strength to fight

So I lay in agony

Longing for daylight

Starlight

My tears shimmer in the starlight
The coyotes' yells ring of fright
Wondering what lies in the silent oppressive night

I am caught now in a plight
Struggling with what little might
I have left to save my soul from sinking with the already disappeared twilight

I wonder where I went wrong
Where everything went so wrong
But through all this wondering
I feel nothing but an overwhelming sense
Of calm

My hands clamp tighter

I feel the surge of peace
It swells, sweet satisfaction filling
Me from bottom to top

The moon weeps, sitting so lonely
It sobs hushed cries and wonders
If only

One thing would have gone differently
If one argument hadn't happened
If one person had kept his lips fastened

But there is no if only
There is only what is
And it will remain now forever
As it is

The struggle slows
The breathing begins to go

The turmoil is at rest
The voices in my head begin to arrest
The balm of final relief washes over me
Of its power I cannot begin to attest

I look down at the quiet eyes
Still twinkling with the waning embers of a final desire for forgiveness

As I keep gazing my heart grows harder

The possibility of forgiveness drifts farther
And farther

A smile spreads across my face
The tears have dried now
Leaving only a dull trace

With his life, all my worries take flight
And not a sound can be heard

Save for the twinkling starlight

The End

It is all the same
In the end
All things crippled and lame
At the end

You've arrived now
At the culmination
Of your journey through
The twisted
Tormented corridors
Of my mind

You've made it through the dark hallways
The clocks ticking
The angels singing
The bells ringing

All the time harassed
By those incessant
Voices inside my head

I am sorry to say
That there is nothing to say
No award that stays
Quietly at the end in wait

There is only the infinite memory
Of the glimpse you've had
Into the darkest trenches of me
Just me

This is the plague
That haunts me
The things that go bump in the night
That constantly taunt me

You cannot return
From this place
It will forever burn
You are now caught eternally in a race

That you can never win

So just let the ever present din
Take hold of you

Let the touch of fire
Become cold to you

Forget the sanity of the world that you know

And in its stead

Just keep listening

To the voices in my head

www.ingramcontent.com/pod-product-compliance
Lightning Source LLC
Chambersburg PA
CBHW070824170726
48000CB00019B/2584